S0-AKQ-137

My Dog, Trip

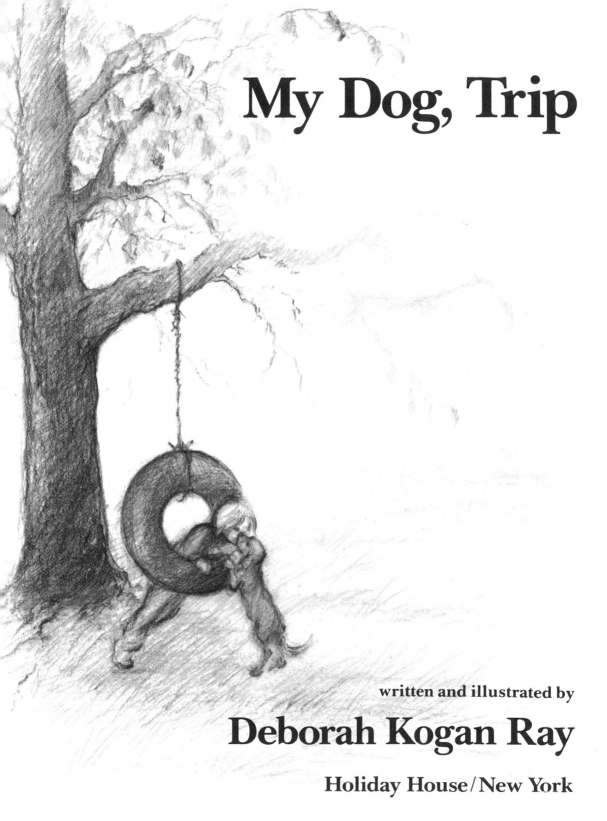

written and illustrated by

Deborah Kogan Ray

Holiday House / New York

For Karen and Nicole, remembering
our dog, Parashka

Library of Congress Cataloging-in-Publication Data

Ray, Deborah.
My dog, Trip.

SUMMARY: A young girl describes her experiences
caring for her orphaned puppy Trip.
[1. Dogs—Fiction] I. Title.
PZ7.R21013My 1987   [E]   87-401
ISBN 0-8234-0662-8

Trip was an orphan dog when I got him. It happened this way. One day, Daddy come home from work carryin' somethin' zipped up in his jacket. When I look inside, I see this rolled-up pup shakin' away. It's so tiny and so skinny, it breaks my heart.

My daddy tells us that the pup's mama was killed by a car up on Coal Creek Road. She was a watchdog at the mine. Daddy say, "Darn fool who run her down didn't tell no one what was done. No one knew she was gone. The watchman went lookin' for her when he saw she hadn't come 'round for her food. It was too late for her pups. They needed their mama to feed them. This little baby's the only livin' one left."

My daddy got a kind heart so he brought the pup on home.

My mama say, "Poor little thing. He
don't look like he got long for this world
neither."

I'm cryin' for hearin' what happened.

I say, "Mama, I'll make him well."

"Allie, don't you set your heart on it,"
Mama say.

But I do.

Mama heats up some milk on the stove
and gives me a baby bottle for to feed him.
Poor little thing's too weak to suck. So I put
drops of milk on my fingers and dribble it
into his mouth.

That night, I keep him warm in a baby blanket, sleepin' with me in my bed. He's so runty, I'm afraid he will die.

But he don't. Not long, and he's drinkin'
from the baby bottle. He's gettin' better
every day. Not long, and he get to look like
a fine healthy pup. Real frisky, too.

Mama's real surprised and real proud of
me.

She say, "That's a lucky pup to have got
you for his mama, Allie."

Daddy's real proud too. I hear him tellin'
how I saved the pup's life to Gramma on
the telephone.

I'm real happy. Pup's so happy, his tail's waggin' all the time. He's growin' big. And he's gettin' the biggest feet. He's always fallin' over them.

One day, I'm helpin' Daddy bring in some firewood from out by the shed. Daddy say, "Allie, you got a name you gonna call that dog of yours? Seems funny just callin' him Pup."

I think and think. I try findin' just the right name. Dogs always called things like Spot or Rover in my readin' books. But Pup don't look like none of them.

I think and think some more.

Settin' dinner, Mama has me puttin' out the mash' potatoes. I'm carryin' them real careful 'cause the bowl so full. Just then, that pup jump up like he ain't seen me in a year. But he trip right over his own big feet. The rug go slidin' this way and that. Me, I go slidin'. Fall right over that dog. Go right down. Mash' potatoes, they go flyin' all over.

Mama hollers at me and throws that pup out the door.

I wouldn't think to cross my mama when her temper's up, but here I am, sittin' on the floor in a mess of mash' potatoes with Mama hollerin' at me, when I break out laughin'. What's popped into my head that's so funny is I've got my name for Pup.

I say, "Mama, from now on I'm callin' my pup Trip. Trip for his trippin'-up feet."

Mama gives a halt to her hollerin'. She looks hard at the mash' potato mess, then she looks squinty-hard at me.

"Allie," she say real slow. "I don't think I ever heard a more fittin' name."

Then she starts laughin' too. Soon we both laughin' so hard that our sides is hurtin', and we still get to laughin' every time we talk about how Trip got his name.

Trip got to be my best friend in this whole world. He help me with my chores. And he always want to play with me. Every day, he's waitin' for me when the school bus lets me off.

One day, Trip ain't there.

I clap my hands and call to him. But Trip don't come. He ain't anywhere in the house neither.

Mama don't remember seein' him since mornin' when she was hangin' wash. I run over to Ginny's house. Trip love rompin' with Lady, her old hound dog.

But Trip's not there.

I run on up Huckleberry Hill so I can look all 'round.

Don't see Trip nowhere.

I cut back through the woods, go all along the creek, up over the bridge out to Coal Creek Road. Go up and back the roadside clappin' and hollerin', "Here, Trip, here."

But Trip don't come.

It's gettin' dark. Cars comin' and goin' fast on Coal Creek Road. I'm afraid of what I'm thinkin'. Could be a car run Trip down.

He could be hurt or dead.

I run home, get Daddy to take me out with the flashlight. I'm so shakin' scared, I hold tight to my daddy's hand. We go a long ways, lookin' with the light.

When we get home, my mama say, "Thank the Lord, Trip wasn't run down out there like his mama was."

Sayin' my prayers, I pray Trip gonna be back when I wake up. But I can't fall asleep for cryin'. Trip's not sleepin' at the bottom of my bed like he always does.

He ain't there in the mornin' neither.

In school, I don't hear when Miss Calley call on me. Can't think of nothin' else for wonderin' will Trip be there when I get home.

I'm waitin' for the school bus door to open when we pull up to my stop. Trip ain't waitin' there. I call for him, but I know it ain't no use.

Mama say, "Come on here, Allie," and she sit me on her lap. She hug and kiss and quiet-talk. But nothin' Mama say can make it be all right.

I don't know what to do.

When Daddy come home from work, he say we gonna make a sign, take it into town and put it on the bulletin board at the market. We write that sign up good. It say LOST DOG and tells all about Trip. Tells his name, how old he is and how he looks. It say he belong to me, Allie Caulfield, and that I love him very much. Tells where we live and our telephone number, too.

Mama say, "Lots of folks gonna see that sign tomorrow, 'cause Saturday's marketin' day."

First thing next mornin', Daddy say we goin' over to help Gramma 'cause she feelin' so poorly with achin' bones.

I don't want to go. I say, "Daddy, someone could call or come by sayin' they got Trip."

Mama say, "Don't worry, Allie, I'll be stayin' here."

I'm worried all the way to Gramma's house.

Gramma say, "What's the matter, where's that Allie smile?"

When I tell her what the trouble be, she say, "Frettin' won't do no good, darlin'. You got to try to take your mind off Trip."

But I can't.

I get to cryin' for missin' him so much.

After visitin' with Gramma, Daddy say we got to go to the hardware store to buy some nails for fixin' the porch.

We stop at the market first. I make sure our sign still there. Then we go to the hardware store.

I'm hopin' Daddy hurry up and buy those nails so we can go home. But Daddy ain't in a hurry. Seem like he gonna take forever jokin' and chattin' with this one and that. Daddy give me money to buy myself a soda from the machine at the garage.

I'm sippin' my soda when Mr. Small the barber come wavin' and callin' to me.

"You Tom Caulfield's girl Allie who lost her dog, ain't you?" he say.

Mr. Small tell me he just saw our sign at the market and how this mornin' when he was cuttin' Joey Welch's hair, Joey was tellin' about a hurt dog he found two days ago when he was huntin' rabbit with his friends. "Dog's at Joey's house," Mr. Small say. My heart's beatin' so hard. That dog got to be Trip.

I run to get Daddy to take me to Joey's house right away. But he don't know where it is. Mr. Small say somewhere back in Brown's Holler. But he ain't sure where. Neither is a lot of folks. We ask and ask before we find someone who know for sure.

We got to drive way back in the holler. Then we get lost up a dead-end road. By the time we find the right house, Daddy's pretty peeved and I'm jumpy as a frog. Daddy rap on the screen door. A lady call out, "What you want?"

"We Tom and Allie Caulfield from over Coal Creek," Daddy say. "We come to see if the dog your boy Joey found belong to Allie here."

"You're welcome to see," Joey's mama say. "Poor thing's in a bad way though. His leg's broke and he's all cut up and feverish. We tryin' to keep him warm."

Daddy go over to a rolled-up blanket by the stove. I scrunch my eyes shut. I'm afraid what I'll see.

"Allie," Daddy say real quiet. "It ain't Trip."

I'm feelin' all mixed up. Part of me is glad that hurt dog ain't Trip.

I cry all the way home.

Get to thinkin' of that poor hurt dog and my stomach gets all knotty. The same thing might have happened to Trip.

A whole week go by.

Nobody call or come 'round sayin' they found Trip. I'm thinkin' Trip gone forever now.

Mama has me shellin' peas for Sunday dinner when the telephone rings. Mama answers, and I hear her sayin', "That's right, sort of brown with real big feet."

"It's Trip!" I yell.

Mama shushes me. She askin' questions. I'm tryin' to hear what they sayin' in the telephone, but I can't. They talkin' a long time.

Mama say, "Thank you. Allie and her daddy be comin' right over to see."

"Is it Trip, Mama?" I ask.

"Won't know for sure until you get there, Allie," Mama say.

"Suppose it ain't, Mama," I say. "Maybe it'll be like last time when we thought we found him."

Mama hug me. "Allie," she say, "it sure
does sound like Trip to me." Mama wink to
me. "That lady went on and on about her
troubles with that dog's trippin'-over feet."

That dog got to be Trip.

I got my fingers and my toes crossed.
Can't stand still while Mama tellin' Daddy
all about how that lady seen our sign up,
what her name is and what roads we got to
take.

Daddy say, "That dog sure did travel a
ways."

Can't sit still the whole way out. Daddy
keep mindin' me not to bite my fingernails.

Finally we turn onto a dirt road. Bump up.

I hear barkin'. Then comin' out from behind the house, I see Trip. He come runnin' and waggin' up to the pickup. I never been so happy to see anyone in my whole life.

I jump out. Trip jump up and lick my face. I hug him and kiss him. I'm laughin' and cryin' same time. He lickin' me, and I'm huggin' and kissin' him some more.

Then Daddy give me a little tug.

He say, "Allie, time you be rememberin' your manners. Come say thank you to these kind folks who been carin' for your dog."

I ain't seen nobody was there but Trip.

Daddy say, "This is Missus Holbrook and her little girl Lizzie."

I hold onto Trip when I shake Missus Holbrook's hand.

"I'm happy you got your dog back, honey," Missus Holbrook say. "Lizzie here been feedin' him and fussin' over him all week. She even got a name for him. Lizzie found him wanderin' down on the road when she went to get the mail. We didn't know where he come from. When I saw your sign at the market this mornin', I told Lizzie that dog Trip sounds just like the one you been takin' care of. We have to telephone those folks and see. Ain't that right, Lizzie honey?"

Lizzie look like she been cryin'. She hidin' behind her mama and holdin' to her hand. She's little, littler than me.

She look at me. I look at her.

I just know she been thinkin' Trip was her dog now. It breaks my heart to see her so sad.

I say, "Lizzie, you can come visit Trip any time you want."

Lizzie make a sort of smile. She come pat Trip. Only she call him Bobo. I ask her to come visit real soon, and her mama say she can.

Daddy and me make our thank yous and good-byes. Trip jump in the pickup and sits himself by the window like he always does. I see Lizzie wavin' to Trip when we drive off, and my heart's still sad for knowin' how bad she must feel.

Ridin' home, I hold so tight to Trip.

I don't never want to let him go.